REBA & KATHERINE
Messy Hair Game

written by
Gail Gritts

illustrated by
Javier Duarte

ENDORSEMENTS

"This delightful story, for the adult reader, might rekindle memories of growing up under the watchful and loving eyes of a grandmother. The young reader will find a lighthearted lesson hidden in this endearing tale of mischief between sisters."

Page Lambert, author of In Search of Kinship, advisor for the Rocky Mountain Land Library.

"Way out at Munson Hill, the rolling, green Ozark Mountains are dotted with cows and horses and hay bales. Not too far past that, you can meander through winding roads to the home where Laura Ingalls Wilder wrote her Little House books. MESSY HAIR GAME is a story about simpler times in the country, in the same spirit as the Little House books. It's a story about fun and family--and a wee bit of mischief. You will love Reba the same way most of us loved Laura."

Lorri Cardwell-Casey is a member of The Society of Children's Book Writers and Illustrators, a former instructor for The Institute of Children's Literature, and writer with more than 550 published stories, articles, and poems appearing in HIGHLIGHTS FOR CHILDREN, HUMPTY DUMPTY'S MAGAZINE, GUIDEPOSTS FOR KIDS, FAMILY CIRCLE, and WOMAN'S DAY. She majored in elementary education, has been a daycare director, and is a mom of four.

Reba & Katherine
Messy Hair Game
2017 Copyright by Gail Gritts
All Rights Reserved

Published by Kids Book Press
An imprint of A & S Publishing, A & S Holmes, inc.
Sharon Kizziah-Holmes – Publishing Coordinator

ISBN: 978-1-945669-38-5

DEDICATION

To my beautiful grandchildren and Grandma Vauna, who
placed her handprint on my heart.

ACKNOWLEDGMENTS

Page Lambert with whom I first shared my dream.

Debra Butterfield who ventured out with me into editing.

Sharon Kizziah-Holmes for being real with me and making the whole process so much fun.

Javier Duarte for bringing Reba and Katherine to life.

Mike Stirrup, my favorite tech-guy of all time, for sorting my media and links.

Keith McHenry, my business manager who assures me it will all be okay.

"Hurrah, we're going to town with Grandma," squealed Reba.

"Well, if you're going with me you must be good girls! Let's get you all cleaned up and ready to go," said Grandma.

"Ouch!" cried Reba, as Grandma combed her long wavy brown hair.

"Be still, sweetheart. We need to look our best when we go to town." Grandma smiled. "There you go. Now come here, Katherine, it's your turn."

Katherine sat still as Grandma sculpted her hair into beautiful curls.

"You look like the baby doll I got for Christmas," Reba said.

"Now, I have to tidy up round here before we head out, so you girls be good and stay clean," Grandma said.

"Can we go outside to play?" Reba asked.

"No," said Grandma, "You'll get hot and sweaty."

"Can we color?"

"No, I'm trying to get things put away, just be patient and sit somewhere quietly," Grandma said.

"Okay. Come on, Katherine, let's go sit under the dining table." Reba called to her little sister.

From under the table, the girls sat watching Grandma flit about the kitchen putting away dishes and wiping down surfaces.

"She's taking forever," said Reba. "Maybe we can play a game while we wait." Then a mischievous idea popped into her head.

"Mess up your hair," she whispered to her little sister.

Katherine grinned and shook her head tossing her curls from side to side.

"You look so funny," whispered Reba and the girls began to giggle.

"What's going on under there?" came the call from Grandma as she peered under the table. "Well, I never. Why did you do that?"

Katherine was silent as Grandma lifted her from beneath the table, untangled her golden locks then sat her back with Reba.

"Just a few more minutes, girls. Please stay clean and tidy," Grandma repeated.

Before long another impish thought took hold of Reba and she again whispered to her little sister, "Mess up your hair."

Katherine giggled ruffling the curls with her fingers.

"You look really funny," Reba said, and both girls broke out laughing.

Grandma stooped down again. This time, her piercing eyes turned toward Reba.

This was not a game Grandma was willing to play.

Dashing from beneath the table, Reba bolted out the back door.

Racing out the door, Reba looked over her shoulder confident she could outrun Grandma.

However, Grandma wasn't running. She was standing by the back door. "Reba, I'm going in to comb Katherine's hair-again. When you are ready to stop this silly game, come back into the house and we will head to town.

Reba hung her head in shame and slowly walked back to the house. "I'm sorry, Grandma. Please forgive me."

"Oh, sweetheart, Grandma will always forgive you."

After a big hug, they headed to town.

And the girls never played the messy hair game again.

About the Author

Gail grew up deep in the heart of the Ozarks where she had a happy childhood full of adventure and enjoyed hearing her grandparents recount family history and shenanigans.

Life led her to England where she and her husband Tom raised their own family of five. While living abroad, they created a vibrant and happy home maintaining family ties as they shared tales about life on the farm and the love of grandparents with their children.

Today, though she still lives in England, she relishes the opportunity to keep the tradition of storytelling, including the mishaps and adventures of Reba and Katherine, with her thirteen grandchildren.

Gail has been a freelance writer for many years writing magazine articles and devotional materials. Reba and Katherine is her first venture into children's books.

About the Illustrator

Javier Duarte is a Uruguayan illustrator born in Montevideo in 1979. For three years, beginning in 1993 he studied graphic advertisement at Pedro Figari School of Fine Arts. He studied caricatures and cartoons in 2000 and 2001 with Professor Luis Haro. In 2002 he begun a new and extensive career at Continental Art Schools with Professor Alvaro Fontana successfully passing the regular course of art and artistic workshops extension (ART TRAINING SYSTEM) until 2013. He's specialized professionally in illustration, portraits, cartoons, comics, storyboards and illustrating children's books (published in USA) and is currently working as a freelancer local and international.

Made in the USA
Middletown, DE
30 November 2017